A Little Wisdom for Growing Up

A Little Wisdom for Growing Up

From Father to Son

JOHN C. MORGAN

Resource *Publications*

An imprint of *Wipf and Stock Publishers*
199 West 8th Avenue • Eugene OR 97401

A LITTLE WISDOM FOR GROWING UP
From Father to Son

ISBN 13: 978-1-55635-308-6

Manufactured in the U.S.A.

Contents

Preface

Dear Jonathan,

I know you don't like it when I give you advice, but I believe you also realize that I care about you and want to save you from the same mistakes I made growing up, which is, of course, silly, because you will make your own mistakes no matter what I write. I'm not sure I can remember a single word of advice my father gave me, which doesn't mean he didn't offer any, but only that I had to learn myself by living. I probably thought he knew as little as you think I do now.

Nonetheless, I have learned some wisdom from having lived so long, even if it took me falling down a few times. These short stories, or fables, drawn from the natural world, are simply ways of sharing a few things I have learned after over sixty years on this fragile planet, both from my own life and the teachings of the world's great philosophers. Maybe they will help you grow up wiser than I was. On the other hand, you may make the same mistakes, but at least you won't be able to say I didn't warn you.

Always remember that I loved you. Grow in wisdom and take care of yourself. It's a dangerous but beautiful world, full of illusions and wonders, but mostly a stage upon which you must find your part to play in the unfolding drama. How you decide your role and how you play it will go a long way toward being wise, and wisdom is what we all hope to have one day.

Love,
Dad

A Note for Teachers and Readers

Reading should be fun and interactive. The stories or fables here can be used in many settings and in many ways. Here are a few suggestions:

1. Read the fables as bedtime stories at home. Read the story first; then ask the child what she or he believes the story means. You can then read my interpretation.

2. Read the stories in the classroom setting using the same process described above. I have used this process in my college philosophy and ethics classes and find students love stories and also the game of suggesting what they mean.

3. Adults and or children can use the stories in classes in congregations or other organizations as a way of teaching values or everyday ethics. I would also suggest having students write their own fables or stories and share them with the class.

Have fun!

The Lion and the Ant

ONCE UPON a time there was a great lion in the forest who always took a morning walk. Out on his path one day he came upon a huge chest, which he pried open with his teeth. He looked inside the chest and found gold. He was not quite sure what to do with it but, being proud, he knew he couldn't ask for help, so he left it there and hurried on his way, not wanting others to realize that their king was so weak.

A few hours later an ant happened to come upon the chest. He, too, saw the gold. But he knew it was far too heavy a load for him, so he hurried home and asked a large army of his fellow ants to help. With their help, the ant carried the chest of gold home where they were able to buy enough picnic food to last a few winters or more.

MORAL: If you find yourself with a heavy load, ask friends to help carry it.

The Rainbow

THE COLORS were fighting again as they fell from the sky.

Yellow said: "I am a royal color, just like the sun that is very powerful indeed. Give me more space to fall!"

But Blue disagreed. "I am the color of sky and water and all that makes people happy. I should become the favorite."

It wasn't long before Green cut in. "I am the essential color of life, of plants and trees and all that means the springtime. The earth welcomes me more than any others."

Red then talked about blood and skies and clay, while Purple suggested robes and sunsets as being best. Orange stood up and announced the morning sun and fading moon, while Brown drew attention to the mud and sands that covered the planet.

The more they argued the more the colors flew apart.

Suddenly the whole sky opened up and a voice made them stop fighting and listen. "I grow tired of your arguments about who is the best. You will never accomplish much if you don't get together."

Just as soon as the voice stopped, the colors found themselves touching as they stretched across the sky. They knew they had formed a rainbow.

MORAL: If you spend all your time thinking you are best, you will soon feel very much alone. But if you touch others, you, too, may become thing of beauty, a rainbow.

The Tortoise and the Human

THE HUMAN loved to tease the tortoise.

"See," said the human, "I can run much faster than you can," as he skipped by.

The tortoise looked up and smiled.

"And I can grasp things with my hands, which as everyone knows is the mark of a higher species," the human said as he plucked a berry from the tree and put it in his mouth. The tortoise just smiled.

"Surely the Creator loves me best," the human said, "at least that's what I read in all our sacred books."

This time the tortoise looked at the human directly. "There is one thing I have that you don't."

"And what could that possibly be?" asked the human, hiding a smile about to form.

"Some of us live to be a hundred and fifty years old," said the smiling tortoise, "which means that long after you're gone, I will still be moving along this path with a smile on my face."

MORAL: If you take the long view, sometimes things will work out after all.

The Mosquito and the Hummingbird

IT WAS a late, bright spring morning when the mosquito and the hummingbird found themselves in the same backyard.

The mosquito was quite taken by how fast the wings of the hummingbird fluttered.

"Tell me, friend," said the mosquito, "how do you manage to fly and yet stand still at the same time?"

"I don't think about it else I would drop to the ground," responded the hummingbird. "That's just the way it is," he said as he returned to the fire bush flower on the clinging vine.

"But don't you ever consider how you manage to do this?" asked the mosquito.

"Look, if I had to count how many times my wings go back and forth, I would soon grow weary and fall down and be swallowed by a cat," said the hummingbird, getting a little angry.

"But, still, don't you ever wonder how you do it?" the mosquito asked again.

This time the hummingbird flew away quickly after telling the mosquito that he couldn't stand any more questions.

The mosquito buzzed and laughed. "Now I have fulfilled my purpose—being irritating."

MORAL: Everyone has some purpose, even if only to irritate others.

The Bee and the Wasp

THE WASP was one very proud insect. He knew that even the threat of a sting from him made humans race away. "Such power, such power," he said to himself as he looked for more humans to scare.

It only took a moment for him to spot a family on a picnic. He went into attack mode, diving toward a child and making her run away. "No one can stand up to me," he laughed to himself with a very wasp-like chuckle that sounded very much like a whizzing noise.

He decided to move in closer to strike terror in the other humans, when he came upon a bee.

"I hope you are not planning to scare these humans away," the wasp said, "because I am louder and more dangerous than you."

"No," responded the smaller bee, "I could sting them, but I choose not to do so. There are other ways to make yourself known."

"And what gets more attention than my loud buzzing?" asked the wasp.

"Well, it is true you get their attention," responded the bee, "but if you look around, you will see all the family have left—which surely must make you feel lonely, not just powerful."

The wasp thought for a moment and then said, "Well, at least I get their attention, which more than I can say for you."

"But you miss my point," said the bee. "I am the insect who gives them honey, so they remember me for a long time after I leave."

So saying, the bee fled to his hive, leaving the wasp wondering why he suddenly felt so lonely.

MORAL: You can keep the attention of others much longer with honey than with a sting.

A Star, a Tree, and a Bird

THE ROBIN sat on a limb of the evergreen tree. He watched the night sky.

"Look at that shooting star!" he sung, wishing he could have half the star power.

The evergreen tree also wished to be more, remembering how the other trees put on coats of red and yellow and orange as the fall turned into a wild display of colors.

Winter soon arrived. There were few shooting stars to be seen. The once proud trees had lost their colors and were brown and bare. The robin returned to a branch in the evergreen tree.

Noon soon came. The sun shone brightly in the pale, grey sky. "How much more beautiful is the sun than all the shooting stars," said the robin. Then, looking at the needles of the evergreen tree, he thought how marvelous their color against the winter whiteness. So saying, he threw out his chest and sang a wonderful winter song that made the tree glad.

MORAL: Don't judge your own beauty by how others look. Just be glad to be you.

Big Fish, Small Fowl

ONE DAY a great whale was sunning herself not far off shore. Along came a seagull, flying lowly overhead.

"My, my," said the seagull, what a great creature this whale is. How marvelous to be so large and command such respect, while I, small and weak, seem but a speck against the sky."

The whale looked up and spotted the seagull. "Oh, oh, how wonderful it must be to be free to fly wherever you want and not be imprisoned by water. I would give anything to be a seagull."

The seagull flew off into the clouds. The whale turned and headed back out to sea.

MORAL: Never compare yourself to others; you'll either feel inferior or superior, and neither attitude will win you friends.

The Caterpillar

THE CATERPILLAR wiggled with great difficulty in his own little home, barely able to move. He grew increasingly depressed thinking about his situation.

"I am doomed forever," said he, crying out to the Creator to be put out of his misery.

The Creator knew better: Things are not always what they appear to be.

"Imagine you are the most beautiful of all my creations, more wonderful than a fall day, more pleasing to the eye than a morning glory on the vine," spoke the Creator.

The caterpillar imagined himself to be just what the Creator spoke. He fell asleep and dreamt.

One day, sitting quite still in his small home, the caterpillar felt himself changing. "This is interesting," he said, looking up to see a small hole in the roof of his home.

Then, in the twinkling of an eye, the caterpillar was free. He floated in the morning breeze and said hello to the morning glories. He watched his amazing black and orange wings fluttering in the breeze, surprised at how graceful he had become.

Is this a dream, he asked himself, or am I completely changed? It didn't matter really; he was just enjoying himself now.

MORAL: Believing is seeing.

The Crows

THE CROWD of crows perched on the farmer's fence. They were hungry, but they also were afraid because right there in the middle of the corn field was the farmer, his arms out to warn them not to eat on his property.

"If that farmer weren't there, I'd fly down right now and have a feast," said one bragging crow.

"Me, too," said another, fluffing out his wings to look bigger than he actually was.

"I've a good mind to fly down on that farmer's hat," said the third crow.

But none of the crows moved, except from time to time to fly away from the field, returning to see if the farmer was still there. "He's one stubborn man," said one of the crows.

"Maybe if we wait until it gets dark, the farmer will be as hungry and tried as we are, and go home," said one crow, shifting his position on the fence.

The crows waited. And waited. And waited. But by the light of the moon the farmer looked even more scary with his arms casting a long shadow across the field.

Morning came. The crows had had enough. "That farmer will never leave," said one, as they flew off in search of a better corn field.

After eating his breakfast, the farmer came out of his house and went into the field to put more straw into the scarecrow's chest, glad to keep his crop safe.

MORAL: Your worst fears may be wrong.

Pink Elephants

Two CATS went for a walk in their neighborhood.

"Have you ever seen a pink elephant?" asked one of them.

"No," said the other, "because there are no pink elephants."

"Of course there are," said the other.

"Ain't so," taunted the second cat.

The first cat stopped for a moment before speaking. "Tell you what—I want you to stop thinking about pink elephants, since according to you they aren't real. Whatever you do, don't think about pink elephants."

"That should be easy," said the other cat.

All day long he tried to stop thinking about pink elephants, but all day long that's all he could think about. He thought about them so much that he began to believe they were real, and when at night he fell into an exhausted sleep, he dreamt about . . . you guessed it, pink elephants.

MORAL: Just let go. The harder you try to get rid of some ideas or people, they more they hang around.

The Wood Thrush's Song

THE WOOD thrush was very scared and quite hungry, so he let out a cry that other birds might hear. The note split the air with its harshness. All the other birds flew away.

One day the wood thrush saw a sunflower growing so high that it touched the branch on which he was perching.

"What a magnificent show," he said to himself. "I must do something to show my appreciation!"

He tried clapping, but there was no sound. He flapped his wings, but he only managed to stir the air around him.

Suddenly, without thinking, he felt within himself a deep joy he had never felt before, so he let it rise from within until he couldn't help but release it. And one of the most beautiful sounds he had ever heard echoed across the woodlands. He thought it was the song of angels, until he realized that when he stopped, so, too, did the song.

"It's me! I am the songbird!" The wood thrush looked down at the sunflower and sang again a song of great praise.

MORAL: Joy may be brief, but it is worth living for such moments.

The Crocodile's Dilemma

MOST FOREST creatures consider the crocodile to be the meanest of all who inhabit their world.

Mothers often will tell their children never to go near the water for too long and especially not to wade too deep into rivers where the crocodiles might live or else a monster could leave teeth marks in their necks.

One day a baby bunny was told never to get too close to the water, but when he heard about the monsters he was curious, not afraid. One day he ventured close enough to the edge of the water to speak with a crocodile.

"You are an amazing creature," said the bunny, "but I am smart and won't get any closer because I know you would eat me."

"A wise warning," said the crocodile, whose eyes were peering at the bunny.

"But I am better at something than you are," challenged the bunny.

"And what could that possibly be?" bellowed the crocodile, convinced that such a harmless creature could do little better than he could.

"I will challenge you to do something after I do," said the bunny, "and if I win, you have to promise never to eat me."

"You're on," said the crocodile.

The bunny paused and then spoke: "All you have to do is say something I say and pronounce it correctly: The thunder thrashed against the tiny tigers."

"That's not hard," said the crocodile, as he tried to say the sentence. But no matter how hard or how long he tried, he just couldn't repeat the sentence correctly.

The bunny repeated the sentence correctly.

"Tell me, bunny," said the crocodile, "how did you know I would not be able to say this sentence?"

"Easy," replied the bunny. "I was told by other creatures that you cannot move your tongue, and I figured you'd never be able to say 'the thunder thrashed against the tiny tigers.'"

The crocodile laughed and swam away, but not before saying: "A deal is a deal. I won't eat you."

MORAL: Sometimes knowledge is better than brute strength.

The Skunk's Kingdom

ALL THE creatures of the forest had gathered to vote on who would be king for the year.

As with humans, so with animals—in crowds they sometimes argue and have to be stopped from hitting one another.

The lion argued that the strongest should rule, for, he said: "If we are ever attacked, I will lead our troops into battle!"

The beaver responded that he had a better idea; he would build a dam around the forest so that no one could get in. The wasp replied that his army would sting any invaders before they set foot in the kingdom.

The animals took a vote and it was split. No one had a clear majority of the votes. The monkeys even claimed the voting was fixed; the elephants replied that they would never forget this day of injustice.

After a tenth vote, the animals were restless. Finally, the skunk spoke out: "My friends, I have only a few words, but I will illustrate what might happen if anyone entered out kingdom to hurt us." At which point, he lifted his tail and released a tremendous fume of ill smelling fluid. All the animals scattered. The skunk found that he was now alone.

"I cast a vote that the skunk rule for a year," he said. And then he voted before declaring: "The vote is unanimous. I rule." He chuckled and went on his way.

MORAL: In politics, as in life, it is not always what you say, but how you say it that wins the crowd.

Pigeon Control

THE HUMANS were at it again, trying to find a way to rid themselves of pigeons who often dropped their you-know-what on anyone below them.

The humans tried loud noises with high frequency waves, but still the pigeons stayed.

The leaders were embarrassed; the people were angry and wanted action.

At one night meeting, they leaders were about ready to appoint a team to shoot the pigeons from their perches, until one person stood up and suggested a better way. Someone in the back said it made sense to try something different before resorting to violence.

The next day the human found a pigeon on his window sill and said to him: "We will train you to go out to sea to find people who are lost, if you will agree to find perches outside the city."

The pigeon went back to his group and said this was a good deal for everywhere, far better than other deals. All this pigeons flapped their wings of approval, and the agreement has lasted to this very day.

MORAL: You don't have to resort to violence to resolve most disagreements; sometimes, all you need do is talk.

The Tiger's Hunger

"MY MOUTH is bigger than yours," bragged the tiger to the hummingbird hovering in front of him. Secretly the tiger thought to himself that even a small bird might silence his hungry tummy.

"That's true," replied the hummingbird, "and, I suppose, if you wanted, you could eat me in a second. I also suppose you have a very big stomach and a tiny morsel such as me would not have made a dent in your dinner menu."

"Quite right!" growled the tiger, as he walked away to find a bigger meal.

The hummingbird breathed a sigh of relief as his heart slowed down to 1,400 beats a minute.

MORAL: It's all how you perceive things.

The Grand Ant

THE ANTS were meeting to select their new leader, but no one wanted the job.

Though many ants knew it would be an honor to lead, most of them were used to working together and didn't want the job which mainly required the leader to take criticism, eat, and grow fat.

The meeting had gone on for hours until one small ant said he would tackle the job if others would lead with him. The other ants had never heard of such an arrangement, but after a vote of many legs, the decision was made with everyone voting in favor. No ant decision is ever made without everyone approving. The other ants said they would help, but also that they would call the leader "The Grand Ant."

Many ant generations have passed since this decision was made. The ants now change leaders every year so everyone gets a chance at the job, realizing that other than a title (like the King or Queen of England), the job doesn't require much work but does wonders for the colony.

MORAL: "Go to the ants . . . , consider her ways and be wise" (Proverbs 6:6).

The Panda's Delight

THE TINY squirrel pleaded with the panda bear: "Please, sir, don't eat me! I will do anything you want if you spare my life!"

"I don't desire to eat you," replied the panda.

"How can that be?" asked the squirrel, remembering that all the bears he had watched before would have eaten him quickly.

"I just don't desire to eat you. In fact, I don't desire much at all right now except to be left alone to enjoy my lunch." So saying, the panda turned to munch on bamboo shoots.

The squirrel thanked the panda and ran away, suddenly remembering that his mother had once told him that the panda only ate vegetables, as he should, too.

MORAL: Having few needs makes life more simple.

The Great Sun

THE GREAT Sun looked down on the planet and smiled. He was powerful, his breath so hot that he could melt ice or cause the creatures below to seek shelter.

"Who should I smile down on today?" the sun thought.

He looked upon continents and across oceans. He viewed cities and villages for someone to smile upon. Then he spotted a few humans in a field. "I shall visit them with my breath," he boasted.

Just when he was about to smile, a dark cloud moved in front of him, blocking his view of earth and giving the humans protection.

MORAL: A lot of life is a matter of timing.

The Great Meeting

THE CREATURES of the forest had called a general meeting to discuss the humans, who were taking over the planet and making a mess of things.

"Why must these humans destroy everything they touch?" asked the zebra.

"Well, for one thing, their brains are small," said the giant ape. "They seem to lack the most basic wisdom of all—to live in harmony with the great web of life. You would think it might dawn on them, but I am afraid they will only learn when it is too late."

"And they kill more than they can possibly eat!" exclaimed the tiger.

"And they even kill their own kind over words," responded the turkey vulture.

"They seem unable to do much without machines," said the turtle dove, "so maybe they have forgotten what it means to survive on their own."

The owl spoke: "And how do you suppose they got their machines?"

The other animals waited because they knew the owl was so smart that he never asked a question unless he had an answer already prepared.

"A little thumb, that's all. A little thumb helps them grasp and make things and hold unto branches . . . and weapons, too. Without the thumb, they would be nothing."

"Are you saying we should steal their thumbs?" the peacock asked, as the other animals giggled.

"No, it's more than the thumb actually. The humans also walk upright because they have so many bones in their feet. But some of us walk upright, too, so that can't be the reason."

21

The owl grew silent. For once he didn't seem to have the answers.

"So what can we do to keep them from destroying our planet?" asked the elephant.

The owl thought for a moment and finally spoke: "Alas, my friends, despite their thumbs and brains and feet, these humans don't seem to learn much from their own mistakes; they just keep repeating them. One day they will have such power that they will make a bigger mess of everything than they already have."

The animals grew quiet. No one spoke. A great silence settled over the forest.

Somewhere in the towns and cities of the humans, a few felt the silence and bowed their heads.

MORAL: Hope is possible if only a few feel their connection to everything.

The Queen of Flies

THE FLIES were very unhappy. "We are not very attractive," one said as he dove into a waste can to eat a leftover piece of celery. He got stuck and had to slide around in the muck before flying away.

"Who would ever want to be like us?" said another, as he fly out of the way of a backhanded swat by a human with a rolled up newspaper in his hand.

Suddenly, from above, they all thought they heard the whirl of wings, but no one saw anything.

"I sure felt something," said one fly as he glanced upward.

"What was that?" said another.

"I have no idea," responded a small fly.

Whatever it was, the flies still tell stories about that day because they believe they had witnessed something quite wonderful, something that made them proud for some reason they didn't quite understand, something that felt like a great message from above.

Though the flies would never know it, on that particular day a dragonfly had flown over them.

MORAL: There is always something greater in you than you know.

The Starfish and the Monkey

THE PLAYFUL monkey decided to visit the ocean. So one summer day he packed up some bananas, a ball, a rope, and headed off the beach to have fun.

"Wait 'til I show off all the tricks a monkey can do!" he exclaimed.

In a few hours he came over the ridge of sand dune and there before him stretched the greatest body of water he had ever seen. "It even plays like I do," said the monkey, noticing the waves splashing on the sandy beach.

"I can show this ocean a thing or two," he said. He bounced the ball, jumped rope, and made monkey faces at the waves.

The monkey stopped playing and glanced down to see a most marvelous creature shaped like a star.

"Who are you?" asked the monkey.

"They call me a starfish," said the creature.

"Want to see me jump rope?" said the monkey.

"No thank you," responded the starfish, "as I am waiting for the tide to come in and take me out to sea."

"Want to see me bounce the ball off my nose?" asked the monkey, getting a little upset because the starfish was not paying attention.

"No, thank you," the starfish responded.

"I can do many things to amaze you; that's why I live—to amaze people with my tricks."

"I can do only one thing," said the starfish.

"Sorry to hear that," said the monkey. "You must be sad."

"Perhaps, so," the starfish responded, "but I am the only creature able to do this one thing."

"That is impossible," the monkey responded, believing he could match anyone.

"Watch closely," said the starfish as he turned his stomach inside out.

The monkey thought and thought. As the tide took the starfish back to sea, the monkey grabbed his ball and rope and headed home.

MORAL: Doing one important thing really well is better than doing a lot of things poorly.

The Land without Snakes

THE SNAKES believed they could live anywhere. And so they slithered throughout the world, sneaking on big ships to cross the seas, and occupying new lands where no other creatures had gone.

"We are the kings of all we survey," boasted the chief snake before a large gathering of the annual convention of worldwide adventurers.

"There is a place I would wager you could not live," said a mole after the speeches.

"And where might that be?" responded the snake, as if challenged.

"Probably in my homeland," said the polar bear standing nearby.

"And where is that?" asked the snake.

"Antarctica," said the bear, explaining to the snake that he could not crawl across the bitterly cold ice very long.

The chief snake gathered the other snakes together to see if he should slink to Antarctica and give it a try. After all, snakes don't take "no, you can't do that" very well as a final answer.

But, after much debate, all the snakes agreed that Antarctica was a place they didn't want to go.

So they slinked and slivered out of sight.

MORAL: There are some lessons better not experienced.

The Human Body

THEY WERE at it again. Their cries echoed throughout the forest until the animals started to leave in order to find peace and quiet elsewhere.

"These humans," said the elephant who never forgot such things, "they do nothing but argue among themselves as to which one is the greatest, which one has the best God, nation or language."

"Yes," said the deer softly, "and now even the parts of the human body are fighting." So saying, she darted away.

The animals listened.

"I am number one!" thundered the ears, "because without us these humans cannot hear one another."

"With you around, that might be a blessing," quipped the nose, sniffing the air with great zeal. At least I give these humans a sense of smell."

"None of you is as important as we are," said the eyes, "because without us these humans bump into trees."

None of the body parts noticed the fingertips as they touched the mouth. "But we are the most sensitive of all, and right now we are going to leave the body and go somewhere else!"

So saying, the mouth and fingertips left, leaving the others to figure out how to argue without having a mouth or fingers to point.

The forest animals breathed a sigh of relief.

MORAL: Everyone has a part to play in life.

The Duck and the Owl

IT WAS noon; the owl was trying to sleep in the branches of his favorite tree, but he was awakened by loud quacking below. He opened one eye and saw a duck waddling down the path, her head bobbing back and forth, as if she were arguing with herself.

The owl studied her carefully, as was his practice. "She seems to be alone, yet she continues to quack and nod her head as if in some debate."

"Excuse me, madam duck," hooted the owl, being sure the duck would want words of wisdom. But the duck keep on her way, not noticing the owl above.

The owl said again: "Excuse me, madam duck, but if you don't listen to me, I think others will believe you are crazy."

"Well," said the owl as he went back to sleep, "ducks are crazy. They pay no attention to others and don't want advice. I might as well doze off."

Later that night when a few owls were gathering on the branches of the tree, the owl told the story of the duck. One of the older and wiser ducks fluffed his feathers before responding:

"Why, don't you know? A duck can't walk without bobbing its head."

MORAL: Never assume you know much about anyone from their appearance.

The Hobbyhorse

THE MACHINES decided the humans had become out of date. So they simply decided to do away with them.

"All we really need is a way to get around the city without them," said one machine. The others agreed and so began a plan to provide each machine with transportation.

"We must find something cheap to build and easy to use if every machine must have one," said one.

"And it must be good for the world around us else we end up making a mess of things," said another.

The machines went to work, by day and night because, unlike humans, they needed neither food nor sleep. For forty days and forty nights they worked non stop, until finally they had build what they considered to be a perfect machine.

"What shall we call it?" asked one.

"I say we call it a hobbyhorse," countered another.

And so the first machine created by and for other machines was built and named.

"It is a fine machine," said a small toaster, "but it seems to me we need a human to make it move before we can use it."

All the other machines stood motionless and speechless because they knew the toaster was correct.

MORAL: Great projects often fail for lack of planning.

The Clown Fish

THE CLOWN fish were playing again, for that was their role in life.

"Say, have you heard the joke about the flounder, the whale and the shark," said one clown fish, as he burst out laughing before he could finish the story.

"There's something fishy about that joke," laughed another clown fish.

"No, seriously, folks, take my clown fish!" replied the first.

"We really have a problem here, friends," said another, "and it's no laughing matter."

"Problems are simply answers we haven't come up with yet," said the fish known as The Wise One, for he was often serious while the others played.

"It seems we are running out of male fish," said a smaller fish, "and while they may not be good for much, they certainly have a big role to play in our future."

"Not so big a problem," replied The Wise One.

"You see," she continued, "ages ago we were created quite differently from other fish. We were born to change from being males to females and back again if we so desire."

"You mean that any one of us can change into a male?" said the small fish.

"That's it precisely," said The Wise One as she changed into a male.

MORAL: Nature knows more than we do.

Beavers and Bears

THE OTHER animals knew how vicious the great brown bear who ruled over them was. "He's been known to toss you against his cave just because you said the wrong thing or moved the wrong way," said the raccoon.

"How can we continue to enjoy life if we fear him so much?" asked the beaver.

"I agree, but what do you propose doing about the situation?" the squirrel asked.

"Leave it to me," replied the beaver, "because I know the bear's secret."

The other animals did not have the courage to tell the beaver he was no match for the great bear, but they watched as he enters the bear's cave. They expected to hear him cry for help. But it was quiet.

A few moments passed. The animals waited. The beaver finally appeared. "I have spoken to the bear and he has agreed to behave more kindly in the future," said the beaver.

The creatures were amazed, and waited for the beaver to speak.

"I reminded the bear that many ages ago, beavers were about his size, but the Creator, seeing how unfairly we treated others, made us shrink and spend all our time building dams across rivers. He said hard work would make us remember to help others."

MORAL: Speak truth to power.

The Dogs and the Missing Animals

THE ANIMALS were very afraid. Each night, one of them disappeared and no one knew why.

They tried everything to keep themselves safe, but nothing worked. Finally they decided to call a meeting of all the humans and animals to work on a plan of action.

The birds and reptiles presented their ideas, as did the monkeys and ducks. The humans, too, suggested ways to help, but nothing anyone presented seemed possible.

Finally, some dogs spoke up. "Our plan is simple," the collie said, chosen to represent the dog kingdom.

"What we propose to do is have all the dogs circle our country and should a problem arise we will all bark and scare anyone off."

The other animals spoke quietly among themselves first, and then a deer spoke up: "We have nothing to lose. Let's give the dogs' proposal a try."

That night was quiet; not a bark was heard. In the morning the animals gathered again.

The collie spoke: "We circled the country all through the night and found out that no one is coming in to take animals away; they are simply leaving by themselves to go elsewhere."

"Of course," laughed the rabbit, "why didn't we think of that?"

"Because you were thinking the worst without really knowing anything," said the collie.

MORAL: Don't make assumptions until you've checked out the facts.

Letting Go

THE BUTTERFLY held onto the branch with all her might for she was afraid of falling to the ground below. It is a long way to fall and I shall probably hurt myself or even die, she thought to herself.

A bird perched on the branch above had been watching her for some time. "Why don't you just let go?" the bird asked.

"Because I will surely die," said the butterfly.

"That's ridiculous," the bird chirped, "don't you know you can fly?"

"Fly? What's that?" responded the butterfly.

"For me, it's soaring through the air, but I bet with those wings you have you would just float down to the earth below, or, if you decided, you might also fly to another branch," the bird said.

"I'm afraid," replied the butterfly, holding on for she thought was dear life.

"Just let go. Let me count to three and then you let go and float down. If you want, I will fly beneath you just to make sure you have a cushion."

The bird counted to three and the butterfly let go. Catching a small breeze, she floated away.

MORAL: Sometimes you just have to let go to move on.

Footprints

THE KOALA bear paused and looked at her footprints on the ground. "My, how wonderful are these marks I leave."

She bent down to place her paws in the mud, amazed to see the prints that remained. "It's just like the human children do when they leave their handprints in the mud, as if to say: 'Look, I was here!'"

The bear put her paws in the mud again. "One day, a long time from now, someone will walk by and wonder just what kind of creature left these prints!"

MORAL: Everyone wants to leave their mark on the world.

Dung Beetles

By the light of the silvery moon the beetles made their way across the earth's crust. That is how nature made them—to use the pale waves of lunar rays to sense the direct path to the dung nearby, which was their main source of food.

"We may not be very attractive to others," said one beetle, "but when I see us glow in the moonlight, I know how beautiful we really are."

"Yes, I agree," said another beetle, as he followed the light of the moon.

"It makes me want to croon by the light of this silvery moon," said another beetle as he hit a high note.

"We are very marvelous creatures, indeed," echoed hundreds of other beetles.

MORAL: Everyone is beautiful, in their own way.

The Canine Corp

THE DOGS, wolves, and foxes were meeting to talk about how to deal with the humans who were destroying the land.

"I vote that by the light of the moon we attack them and drive them out of our kingdom!" exclaimed one wolf.

The clever foxes thought for a moment before responding: "I think they will only punish us if we try this, and soon there won't be any of us left. Perhaps we should wait it out and hope they grow tired of fighting over who owns what piece of land."

The dogs barked and said: "I suppose they have become my friends. I know their weaknesses, but I also know that not all of them are bad. Maybe we should try to teach them some respect for the earth."

"You say they treat you kindly?" questioned the wolf. "They put you in cages or tie you up outside. Doesn't seem friendly to me."

"And is not the case that when you lose a human, you are taken to a place and left there; and if no other human comes for you, they kill you!" The wolf huffed and puffed more.

"That is true," responded the dog, "but they also feed and care for us and we for them, and there are times when we sit together by the fire that I think of the humans as brothers and sisters."

The wolves and foxes said nothing as the meeting ended, and the dogs went home to their human companions. Nothing was decided.

MORAL: Friends are life's greatest treasures.

The Powerful Elephant King

THE ELEPHANTS were the most powerful creatures in the forest, and their king ruled everyone.

But one morning the monkeys in the trees began to tease the elephants. They loved to play.

"You think you are the most powerful of all creatures, but you're not," said one monkey as he picked a flea off his back.

The elephant glanced up and said: "But I am the most powerful and no one denies it."

The monkey looked down. "If I could find another animal more powerful than you, would you step down as king?"

The elephant roared: "Find such a creature by noon and I will test my strength right here."

The monkey swung down from the tree.

At noon the king elephant rose proudly to proclaim: "See, it is as I told you: I am the most powerful creature of all. No one will come to test me."

He had no sooner spoken than the monkey appeared with a small human child.

The elephant laughed. "You bring me this creature which I can destroy with one foot?"

"You may be strong, but not in everything," said the monkey quietly.

He walked up to the elephant with the child. "I did not say how the contest would be judged, but now I will. Which either one of you can jump highest off the ground will be declared the winner, because as everyone knows it takes great strength to lift your entire body off the ground without help from anyone."

The elephant tossed his trunk by and forth, and pre-pared to lift himself off the ground. But no matter how hard he tried, he couldn't get his entire body off the ground. Panting and tired from the effort, he turned to the child. "Okay, it's your turn; you can't possibly do more than I can."

The human child laughed and jumped once, then twice off the ground. His whole body rose off the earth below.

"You have won," said the elephant as he left.

The monkey smiled a knowing smile and patted the child on the head, on which a crown would have been far too large to place.

MORAL: The contest is not always to the strongest, but to those who use their minds.

In the Beginning

IN THE beginning there was nothing. The whole universe was yet to be.

But the One who brings everything into existence was lonely.

So out of the Creator's breath wind arose and swirled around, doing a great dance of joy to have been freed.

But it was not enough for the Creator.

So out of the belly of the Creator arose flames, darting in all directions, joining in the wind's dance. But still the Creator was lonely.

So gathering the wind and flame, the Creator imagined water flowing everywhere until it dampened the dance of the wind and flame.

The Creator then looked at what was left and blew into the waters the gift of life—small creatures which at first swam but then finally crawled onto the beaches.

"There still is more to come," said the Creator. Bending down to mix together water, earth, fire and air, the Creator gave form to a human being and planted deep within the desire to live and love everything created.

The Creator then laughed and pronounced creation good, if not perfect.

That is how it all began and hopefully will continue as long as humans remember just how important they are to the Creator.

MORAL: Remember you were created for greatness.

About the Author

John C. Morgan is a writer who also happens to teach college philosophy and ethics. He lives with his wife, son, three cats, and one dog—sources of support and learning for his stories. He has written many serious books before, but he believes he had the most fun writing this one. He thinks it may just be his best because it took him over sixty years to learn much at all and then put what he learned into so few words. These stories are intended for children of all ages.